For the three newest Sanders buckaroos: Madi, Jack, and Libby
—R.S.

For Cole, Eli, and Abel with love
—J.M.

Text copyright © 2012 by Rob Sanders
Illustrations copyright © 2012 by John Manders
All rights reserved.
Published in the United States by Golden Books, an imprint of Random House Children's Books,
a division of Random House, Inc., 1745 Broadway, New York, NY 10019. Golden Books, A Golden Book,
and the G colophon are registered trademarks of Random House, Inc.
randomhouse.com/kids
Educators and librarians, for a variety of teaching tools, visit us at randomhouse.com/teachers
Library of Congress Control Number: 2011938519
ISBN: 978-0-375-86985-3 (trade) — ISBN: 978-0-375-96985-0 (lib. bdg.) — ISBN: 978-0-375-98122-7 (ebook)
PRINTED IN CHINA
10 9 8 7 6 5 4 3 2 1

Cowboy Christmas

By Rob Sanders

Illustrated by John Manders

A GOLDEN BOOK • NEW YORK

"Three days till Christmas," said Dwight.

"And we're stuck with cows," whined Darryl.

"Santy Claus will never find us out here on the range," sniveled Dub.

Cookie stirred the beans.

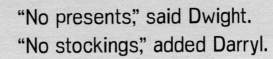

"No presents," said Dwight.
"No stockings," added Darryl.
"No Santy," groaned Dub.

"Time for supper, cowhands," Cookie called.
The cowboys hunkered down 'round the campfire.
Cookie doled out plates.

"When I was knee-high to a grasshopper, my daddy chopped down an evergreen for our Christmas tree," said Dwight. "We decorated that tree with popcorn, and icicles as shiny as silver spurs."

"*You* could decorate a tree," mumbled Cookie, spooning up beans and corn bread.

"That's a fact!" shouted Dwight.

"We'll help," said Darryl.

"Santy loves Christmas trees!" whooped Dub.

Dwight lassoed the only tree he could find—a cactus.

Darryl hauled in hay-cicles.

Dub corralled cans of corn. "No corn popper," he explained.

Then the cowboys hung decorations and stood back to admire the Christmas cactus.

"Ain't much," Dwight admitted.

"Downright ugly," Darryl cracked.

"Santy cain't put presents under that," Dub groaned.

"Off to bed, cowpokes," said Cookie.

The next day, the cowboys roped steers, wrestled longhorns, and wrangled up strays.

That night, they circled 'round the campfire again.

"Every Christmas," Darryl began, "Granny baked cookies, then heaped on sticky frosting and sugary sprinkles."

"*You* could make sugar cookies," muttered Cookie.

"Straight shootin', I could!" hollered Darryl.

"We'll lend a hand," offered Dwight.

"Santy loves cookies!" hooted Dub.

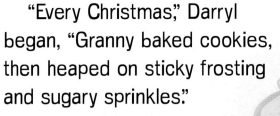

Darryl mixed, rolled, and cut out cookies, then fried them to a crisp.

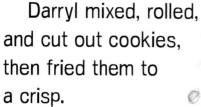

Dwight frosted the cookies with sticky molasses.

Dub added beans. "No sprinkles," he explained.

The cowboys sampled the charred sugar-molasses-bean cookies.

"Don't taste like Granny's," Darryl gulped.

"Downright awful," said Dwight.

"Santy ain't gonna like 'em," Dub fussed.

"Off to bed, cowpunchers," ordered Cookie. "Tomorrow's Christmas Eve."

The next day, the cowboys headed for high country, herded bovines, and haggled with misfits.

That night, they moped 'round the campfire.

"I remember," said Dub, "when Pa turned our hay wagon into Santy's sleigh and Momma stitched reindeer costumes for the horses."

"*You* could do that," Cookie murmured, dishing up apple pie.

"Darn tootin'!" Dub yelped.

"Not with our horses, ya don't," warned Dwight.

"That goes double for me," added Darryl.

Dub lashed twigs to the herd's heads, tied bandannas
to their tails, and dangled cowbells 'round their necks.
Then he stood back and took a gander.

"Those heifers look ridiculous," said Darryl.
"Downright pitiful," Dwight agreed.
"Nothing like Santy's reindeers," Dub sniffed.

"Off to bed, cow wranglers," Cookie called. "Tomorrow's Christmas, and my day off."

On Christmas morning, the cowboys drove the cattle out to graze.

"Another day, another cow," grumbled Darryl.

"We missed Christmas altogether," Dwight griped.

"Santy Claus missed *us* altogether," whimpered Dub.

The cowboys spent the day mending fences, minding the herd, and feeling low-down and miserable.

Near sunset, the boys rounded up the cattle and moseyed toward camp.

"Hey! Did y'all just hear jinglin' bells?" cried Dub.

"I think I smell something mighty fine," said Darryl.

"Do ya see somethin' glowin' down at camp?" asked Dwight.

The cowboys stared.

The camp looked as pretty as a picture postcard!

"Ho! Ho! Ho!" a voice rang out.
"Santy Claus?" cackled Dub.

"Merry Christmas, boys!" Santa called.

"Yee-haw!" crowed Dub. "Ya found us all the way out here!"

By the light of the Christmas campfire, the cowboys chowed down with Santa, tore open presents, and sang carols 'round the tree.

Later, after Santa had disappeared into the night with a jingle and a jangle . . .

. . . Cookie galloped back into camp.

"You missed a rip-roarin' good time," said Dwight.

"And Santy!" gushed Dub.

"Ya don't say," drawled Cookie as he settled near the campfire.

Dwight yawned and stretched. "Well, boys," he said with a sigh, "only six days till New Year's Eve."

"And we're stuck with cows," moaned Darryl.

"Ya think we'll have a party?" asked Dub.

"Could be," said Cookie. "Could be."